Cosmic Love

AGE IS ONLY A NUMBER (AB SHARED WORLDS)

ARTEMED SULLIVAN

Chapter One

LOOKING OFF INTO SPACE, I think about how I got myself into this situation yet again. Why I've *yet again* committed to writing another short story. I'm terrible at this, my writing is so rudimentary it's not even funny. Why do I do *this* to myself? I try and chase the thoughts away. This will pass, I tell myself. It always does, but nonetheless, the jitters and angst always get the best of me at the start of every new story I write. *Every single one.* At the beginning of each one I say to myself never again, but again, here I am.

Now, staring at a blank page with a blinking cursor, I think, *what is this one going to be about?*

The cursor mocks me by blinking in reply. I type.

I am born.

Well, that's a start, be it an unoriginal start, but at least it's a start. As long as I can puke something out on the page as a beginning, I can go back and fix it. Yes, that's it, I can fix it and make it better just like they did with *The Six Million Dollar* man. They rebuilt him and made him better,

1

didn't they? At least, that's how it was in the show. Smacking the backspace key until I clear the three words I've typed, I begin again.

I hate this. This sucks. Why am I doing this? Ugggghhhhhhhh. asdfjkl;

~~*Now that's better. No, it's not.*~~ Mister cursor still blinks his distain at me. I slap the keyboard again, erasing what I've typed. I try once more.

My tormentor burps with a sound like a hyena having eaten the last of the food.

That sounds better than what was there before. Now where do I go with an opener like that?

"Let's see," I say out loud to myself. Hmm, I need a main character, a protagonist. What's her name going to be? I think back to Anne having told me her middle name is Rachel. Since that time, I've always used a variant of her middle name in everything I write. In this case, I settle on the modern Greek version which is Rachil.

Now for the antagonist, what's his name? I then again think back to Anne and what she'd said her husband's name was. She's said his name was Jose. A quick Google search tells me the Greek equivalent is Lossif.

Screw it. I'm using it.

Now, who is Anne, you might ask. Let me back up a bit. My name is Helen, and I'm a manager at a tech company called Cosmic Bang. We're an internet service provider that provides service for home users. Rhett, our founder and CEO, named us Cosmic Bang because we use satellites and wireless radios to bring the internet into people's homes. Anne is the team's project manager, tech writer, and much more. In a nutshell, she's amazing.

I've been talking to Anne a lot about non-work related things. In fact, I've been talking to Anne about non-work related things *too much*. As in too much for being her manager too much. I'm starting to cross a line and I know it. Anne's passion is writing; she writes sci-fi romance.

Our conversation on writing first happened eighteen months ago. We were going back and forth one day, just exchanging phrases, sentences, and paragraphs as a way to have fun on a terrible workday. Anne was the one who encouraged me to write. She even went so far as to tell me that I was a natural. So now, here I am, staring at my laptop screen trying to write when I should be getting a report done that's due soon.

Right at that moment, my company's chat client alerts me with an audible ding, waking me out of my writing trance. I click over to the program and see a red dot next to Anne's name, signaling that she's the one who's messaged me. I click on her name to read the message.

"How's your writing going?" it reads.

"How do you know I'm writing right now?" I type back.

"I just know," she replies with a female imp face emoji. I smile to myself; how does she do this every time? She always knows when I'm doing something. Anne once told me she has a strong intuition about things. Hers must be on steroids because she's right most of the time.

"It's not," I type back to her with a sad parrot emoji. I continue with, "Nothing will flow out onto the page, and what does is utter garbage." I hit the enter key.

"I'm sure it's not," Anne replies. "You're an amazing writer."

"Ah-hem, that would be you and not me," I reply.

"No, it's true. I wouldn't have told you what I thought if it wasn't true. You know me; I don't do that." My laptop dings as she responds with her encouragement.

"I am not a writer," I say again, hitting the return key.

"Helen, yes, you are. Your words are amazing just like you," she writes back.

"No, that would be you on both accounts." Again, I feel myself inching more toward the line I shouldn't be crossing, and I can't help it. I swallow a lump in my throat just as I hit the enter key. My heartbeat pounds in my chest, all thoughts of what I was writing, or more aptly what I was trying to write, have fled my head in an instant.

Is she flirting with me, or just being playful and reassuring since she knows how out of my comfort zone writing is? There's a couple of things about Anne that are a sure thing. One, she's always nice. Two, she's always encouraging. Oh, and I'll add a third, she's the sweetest person I've ever known. Maybe that's covered under two but I'm giving it its own bullet point.

Let me back up one more time. Anne and I were on the same team before what we did was spun-off until its own group. When that happened, I was made the manager. On our previous team, we interacted with each other but really didn't talk about anything aside from work. In fact, Anne and I have been working together for well over four years total. Once we switched to a smaller team, we started to talk about non-work things. In fact, we all did. There were four of us in the beginning, myself included.

First it was things like our dogs since three out of the four of us had dogs. Anne has two golden retrievers named Rose and Lilac; my two are a Pomeranian named Eleni and a Yorkshire Terrier named Georgina (Georgie for short). Then, we all started discussing books and television and after that, movies. It felt like we were all one small, tight-knit family. Soon, our topic of conversation switched to the taboo subjects of politics and religion. The more we all talked about various things from food to what we had planned to do that weekend, the closer we all got.

I noticed that I especially had lots of things in common with Anne. For instance, we both really liked *Star Trek* and *Star Wars*. We'd talk about those two things for hours on end. For me, I was old school *Star Trek*, known to the geeks as *Star Trek* TOS (the original series). I'd read some of the older TOS books and some of the older *NG* (*Star Trek: The Next Generation*) when I was younger. She'd read some of the older and new books, so she had me beat there. For *Star Wars*, I'd only seen the movies and maybe read the novelized version of *Return of the Jedi* when I was about ten. I was team original trilogy (*Star Wars* OT). I hated the prequel and sequel movies that had come out. Oh, I'd dabbled in the comics for OT too, but I was a novice.

Anne, on the other hand, had seen all the movies. She didn't outright hate the prequels and had really embraced the sequels. She'd read a ton of the novels (there's a whole universe of *Star Wars* books out there). She'd even read what's referred to as non-canon. When Disney bought LucasFilms and everything related to it, they deemed anything related to *Star Wars* before the acquisition as non-canon. Meaning that any stories (books and comics) before that no longer existed in the *Star Wars* universe. To my awe, she'd also read the comics and understood how all of that worked.

The world of comics is very confusing until it's explained to you by someone like Anne.

After a while, I was in a *Star Wars* book club made up of just the two of us. I was reading the books and comics and watching some of the animated shows in the *Star Wars* universe. It was so new and refreshing to be around a woman who shared with me what some might call an interest in "boy things." We'd talk about how when we were younger that our brothers got the best toys, they got robots and action figures, and we got dolls and frilly items. When in reality, all we wanted were the fun, way cooler, boy toys.

One time we spent the day talking about shows we'd watched when we were kids. I was all about *Electra Woman and Dyna Girl*, *Wonder Woman*, *The Bionic Woman*, and *The Facts of Life*. She watched those along with even older shows like *Space 1999* that I also watched but were before my time. Anne also watched shows in her generation like *Sabrina the Teenage Witch*, *The Fresh Prince of Bel-Air*, *Family Matters*, *The Wonder Years*, *Mad About You*, *Step by Step*, and *The Nanny*.

We had so much in common that I never thought about the fact that Anne was fourteen years younger than me because she liked things of my generation and things before it. She is a grown adult, but she feels like she's from my generation or older. I'd call her an old soul. Hell, she gives me better advice than friends that are older than me.

I snap myself back into the present with a stern reminder that *Anne is married* and happily, I assume. In frustration over my terrible writing and the fact that I need to back up from that line I'm oh so close to, I change subjects.

"I need to get this report I should be working on finished and over to Rhett for his review," I say.

"I know how much you hate doing that quarterly report," she quickly types back.

"It's even worse this quarter, he wants all kinds of new data added to it this time," I respond at in, from my perspective, a snail's pace compared to her rapid-fire typing.

"Ugh! That just sounds like a living nightmare."

"Trust me, it is. I have to grind through all data picking out the new stuff."

"Give me the new data points once you have them mapped out, and I'll get them added to the quarterly report query, so you have them in there for next time."

That's another thing she is: smart and always willing to offer help. She's the person of my dreams and off limits. I caution myself again. *Focus!* She might be everything I'm looking for, but she's not mine to have. She's given her heart to another, and that other is not me. Nor can it ever be.

"That would be fantastic and a huge help for me. Thank you so much," I write back.

"Of course!" she shoots in response.

"See you at our meeting."

"See you then!"

I throw on some Animotion and crank it up. I take a couple of deep breaths and with a giant mental shove I clear my mind of all thoughts surrounding Anne out of my head. Stealing a moment to look out the window of my living room, I watch the waves hit the shore. I look back at my laptop and focus on the task at hand, writing this goddamn incredibly bloated report that's due by tomorrow morning. My boss, Rhett, is a hard man to please; he changes ideas and direction at the drop of a dime. There will be bloody hell to pay if I don't get this in on time.

With a deep sigh, I begin to type.

Lost in thought, I'm startled by the beeping of my phone. Looking over at it, I realize that's it's a minute until my team's weekly meeting. Our weekly is held at four pm Eastern, this time was picked because it was the most reasonable, given that I'm dealing with three different time zones (Eastern, Mountain, and Pacific). I'm on Eastern, Anne is on Pacific, Davit and Christoforos are both on Mountain. The rest of the team can keep it straight; I basically never know what time it is because of this.

Grrrr! I've been so busy trying to get started on my current story and finishing the quarterly report that I never created an agenda for this week's meeting. *Think! Think! Think!* .... *I know!* I'll just do a check-in with everyone about how their goals for this quarter are progressing. I know ahead of time how this will go. Christos will be totally unprepared and stammer through his update, which will have a lot of unfinished tasks. Davit will be right where he should be in the quarter. And Anne, well, Anne will be almost done and working on some other tasks she's discovered that need to be done. Oh, she'll also offer to help Christos and Davit with their work as well. In a nutshell, Anne is the best employee I've ever had.

Problem now solved; it's showtime. I open the Google calendar invite and click on the link for the Google Hangout video meeting link. Checking to make sure my camara and audio are off, I enter the meeting. Immediately, I hear and see the three of them in deep conversation about this TV show called *The Expanse*. I like the show, too. My team is a bunch of geeks through and through. I smile to myself before unmuting and turning on my camera.

"I missed last night's episode so no spoilers please," I say with a smile.

"Mum's the word," Anne says in her oh so sultry voice. "All I'll say is it was soo good; I can't wait for you to get caught up so that we can all talk about it."

"That it was," Davit says with a nod in agreement.

"Unbelievable," is all Christos utters about the topic at hand.

"I probably won't get to it until this week," I reply.

"I think you're going to really like it," Anne says.

"Well, if all of you like it, I'm sure I will, too, especially since Anne approves and says it was a good episode." I'm grinning as I speak the words. "Does anyone have anything before we move on?" My question is met with head shakes of no.

"Awesome! Now to move on to quarterly goals. Christos, how are things coming along with you?"

"Umm… working with engineering on fixing those bugs is going okay," he stammers out.

In reality, it probably means engineering is blowing him off and he doesn't know how to ask me for help.

"Good to hear. Let me know if you get any pushback and need any help," I say with a smile. "Davit, how goes the battle?"

"Smooth sailing. The equipment upgrades I've been working on have been going well overall. Some equipment crashes are requiring techs to go out and fix some stuff, but those haven't been excessive," Davit replies with a smile. I could probably have him help Christos with his projects but then Christos would get lazy and back off like he's done in the past when Davit has helped him.

"Noice! I've been slightly worried about how bad the crash percentage would actually be, but you've totally eased my mind. Let me know if you hit any snags. Anne, how's the field been taking the new processes you've implemented?" Looking at Anne, I smile, trying to not seem like I'm staring and hanging on every word she says. In truth, I am. Plus, I can't stop looking at her eyes. She has the most beautiful and unique eyes that I've ever seen. They're a deep steel blue. The kind that you just want to get lost in.

"No issues at all with the new processes. One hundred percent buy-in from the field. In fact, the feedback I've

9

been getting is they like the changes and feel it makes everything more streamlined." She says all of this with a big smile and her natural sultry voice. I bet she doesn't even realize the effect her voice has on me. With a mental shake, I snap myself out of my almost trance.

"Great news," I say. "I had a feeling they were going to like the changes, but I wasn't completely sure about it. As always thanks for getting the buy-in. I know it was a tough one for sure."

"Of course!" Anne gives her signature response.

"Great work everyone. As always, your hard work is greatly appreciated. Before we wrap things up, does anyone have anything else?" I'm met with another round of heads shaking no.

"In that case, everyone can get some time back on their calendars. Oh, before I forget. Anne, can you stick around for a few minutes, so that I can go over the new reporting metrics with you?" I feel my heart start to beat faster, and my mouth go dry. All coherent thoughts suddenly leave my brain like water rushing down a waterfall. *Stay cool,* I tell myself. I remind yours truly of the line I'm getting close to. *She's three thousand miles away. And married. As well as your employee. This can never happen.*

"I sure can!" she says and adds, "Christos, Davit, I've got some cycles I can spare if either of you need help with anything."

Both of them nod in thanks.

"Bye guys!" We both say at the same time. After they hang up, we both laugh because we've said the same exact thing at the same exact time.

Still chuckling I say, "Let me pull up my list and email it over to you." After completing that I add, "Sent."

I hear her laptop ding.

"Got it!" she says. I watch her face turn into a serious smile as she pulls up the list and starts scrolling through.

"As you can see it's a lot and difficult to find, but I *think* I was able to map which datapoints we'll need going forward. I'd like for you to double-check to make sure that I'm correct and if so, add it to the script as we talked about earlier." Another thing Anne is great about: gently telling people when they've made a mistake or made a wrong choice.

"Hmm, I think this is definitely doable and of course, I'll let you know if I find anything off with things," she says, slightly distracted as she scrolls through the list I've sent her. I notice she's slightly biting the corner of her lip; it's an adorable, subconscious thing. She glances back up at me. "How's the report coming?"

"Almost done. Just need to polish it up really quick." This report is going to be the death of me, I swear.

"And your story?"

With a big sigh I reply, "It's not." I really want to talk about something else besides my story. Writing for me in the time I've been doing it has always been like pulling teeth. I hate doing it, and I'm also unsure why I continue to do it. Inside, I feel Anne is a big part of the reason why. She's always so encouraging with me about it. Plus, I guess if she thinks she sees a writer in me then maybe I am. I just know the whole process is a nail-biting mess for me from where I sit.

"What's wrong?" she asks.

"I don't know where I'm going with it. Or even what voice my characters should have," I say dejectedly. I don't know how many times I've lamented this same subject to her.

"Do you want any help? You know you can use me as a sounding board," Anne says in a gentle and understanding voice. Here she is trying to sincerely help me and all I can do is whine. God, she's just so perfect as a soul.

Why does she have to be married? I ask myself for the millionth time. I shake myself out of my gushy moment.

"Thank you so much for saying that," I reply with an appreciative tone. "I do know, but I think I want to puzzle over this with myself some more before asking for some advice or help."

"You know how to reach me if you want to discuss things or toss around ideas. You *can* do this; I believe in you. As I keep saying, you're a good writer."

"I know, and when I'm ready, I'll definitely ask you for help."

I know inside how this will go. I'll dig my heels in and bang my head against a wall until I'm overwhelmed with common sense and will hit her up for some advice. She'll then instantly jump into action and come to my rescue as my hero in my own living damsel in distress novel.

"Just to reiterate, I *know* you can do this. Just like you have with your other manuscripts," Anne reminds me in a soft yet firm tone. I could listen to that voice all day, every day for the rest of my life.

"Well, at least someone has faith in me since I don't have it in myself." Anne the ever glass-is-half-full type of person. "Not to switch gears, but do we have anything else to talk about?" I have a ton I want to talk to her about, but none of it is work related and would probably inch me up to *that line* again.

"The only thing else I have is that I should have those new datapoints baked into the quarterly reporting script by the end of the week." A slight smile crosses her lips.

"Thank you so much for being willing to take that one on," I say with sincerity. "On that note, I'll give you some time back. Talk to you later." I wave goodbye.

"Bye," she says while waving as we both hit the disconnect button.

Slumping back in my chair with a sigh, I think for a moment about what I wish I had in my life; the wish is for Anne. Glancing back at my laptop screen, I groan and sit up straight and get back to finishing up this report so I can be done with it. Just a bit more then I can send this off and not think about it until next quarter.

Chapter Two

"WHY THE HELL does he decide at eight pm that the
quarterly report should now be in a different format?" I
yell at no one but myself as I feverishly retype the report
into the new format Rhett has settled on. I sent the
report off at six pm our time to only get an email back at
eight stating that he's decided to change the format and
for me to redo it in the new one and have it in his inbox
before midnight. So here I am, typing like a mad woman
at ten at night, trying to get this done so I can get some
sleep.

I hear a ping and see a message appear in upper right
corner of my screen. It's my infatuation sending me a
message.

"Wow, you're working late tonight," Anne types.

"Rhett wants the format of the report to be different.
So here I am redoing it for him. **sigh**," I type back.

"OMG! That's horrible! Do you need any help with
anything?" she types.

"No, I got it. In fact, I'm getting closer to done as we
speak. Hey, isn't it like seven your time? What has you

14

online with work tonight?" In a second message, I quicky add, "Your boss must be militant."

She reacts to my second message with a laughing emoji. Then I see her typing.

"Nothing's going on. Jose is just working late again. So, I decided to check my email really quick. That's when I noticed you online and wanted to make sure that you didn't need any help," she types back.

I probably shouldn't comment on Jose working late again because someone's personal life is their business and SO off-limits in a work environment. Maybe there are money issues; they do live in California. Or perhaps they're saving up to move out of their townhouse and into a single family. It could be a vacation they're planning on taking. There could be a million reasons why he's working late. I know if I had a choice, I'd be running home to Anne as soon as I could. I dive on in and brush the third rail.

As I type, I know I shouldn't be typing what I'm about to send, but I hit enter, anyway.

"He's been doing that a lot lately hasn't he?" I ask.

"Jose likes the overtime," Anne quickly types.

Anne typed that reply super fast—faster than her normal fast. Am I reading too much into this? I try to think of something nice to say.

"I'm sure you can't wait for him to get home."

I feel myself entering prohibited territory as I hit the return key. I shouldn't have typed that. Shouldn't have pried into something that has nothing to do with me. The air grows thick around me. A sense of dread engulfs me. I also begin to waffle between dread and something else. Taking the recompleted report, I attach it to an email addressed to Rhett and hit send. I continue and try to analyze what this other feeling is. Unlike the dread, it's positive. It only takes me a second to realize what it actually is. It's hope. Hope Anne's having marital issues. Hope that I'd have a chance to be with her. As the thoughts leave my mind, guilt consumes me.

I'm a terrible person for wanting the kindest person in the world to be going through something as terrible as marriage issues.

"How's your report coming?" she quickly types back once more, avoiding the previous topic.

"Just hit the send button on it," I reply.

"That must be a big relief to have that done."

"It is, though part of me is sweating that Rhett will email me back requesting more changes." I'm sure I'll wake up with a start in the middle of tonight over it and what I've said to Anne.

"I don't think he will but fingers crossed just in case."

"I need all the help I can get." In more ways than one, I think to myself.

"It'll be fine. I'm sure of it."

"Thanks for the vote of confidence."

"Of course! That's what I'm here for, to build you up."

"I need someone to."

"Helen, as I've told you before, *you are an amazing person.*"

"No, Anne, that's you from head to toe."

I get a blushing face emoji followed by, "I so am not," as a reply from her.

"You totes are!" I quickly type back. Well, my version of quickly which consists of me typing with two, sometimes three fingers.

There's what feels like a pregnant pause before I see three dots signifying that she's typing a reply.

"If I'm so amazing, then why don't I care that Jose perpetually stays late at work?"

Oh! I think to myself. That was so *not* the answer I was

expecting. I subconsciously run my tongue over my lips to moisten them as my mind races a mile a minute before unceremoniously exploding into a million pieces. I'm pretty sure my brain just briefly stuttered to a stop.

As my brain revs back to life, I see various moments with Anne flash through my head. Anne always popping up at all different hours ready to help me. Her talking about Jose being at work so it wasn't a big deal if she helped me brainstorm plot ideas. Did she do all those things because she was just lonely? Or did she do them because she likes me as her boss? As a friend? Or, and this is a *big or*, because she might share the same feelings I have? As I ponder all of these things, I remember that I need to answer her. How long have I been processing these thoughts? A second? A minute? Five minutes? I need to say something to her about this revelation, but what does someone say to a person who just said they didn't care if their spouse was around or not? I hear a ping and glance down at my laptop screen.

"Never mind what I've just said. I should have never said it out loud. I'm sorry I've said something that makes you feel uncomfortable." I see Anne's words.

I take a deep breath and begin to type out a message that turns into a longish paragraph. "Don't be sorry, there's no need to apologize; you haven't said or done nothing wrong. I'm not one to pry, but if I'm being honest, I've thought something might be up lately with you being online during off-hours. I haven't said anything, because it's your personal business. I'm going to take my boss hat off right now and be here as your friend if you need to talk."

I feel myself wavering back and forth from that line and just focusing on being a good friend and coworker to her. I'm on a slippery slope here right now, but I don't care. All I care about is her.

"Thank you for saying that and I really appreciate it," she quickly sends. "I'm still embarrassed about what I've confessed to you. I'm not even sure why I said it, except that I've always felt like I could talk to you. This is going to sound silly, but I feel like I've known you my entire life, like you're an old friend."

I can feel the warmth and emotion of what she's sent come through my laptop and touch my soul. I feel a lump form in my throat at the thought of her maybe having feelings about me that could be similar to mine. I sense myself being torn between divulging my feelings for her versus being the friend she needs right now in this moment.

"And I feel the same way about you. That I've known you for…well, forever. I know I'm your boss, but I've always considered you a work friend, and at times even more than just a work friend, a friend, friend. If that makes any sense?" I hit enter and wait with bated breath, hoping I just didn't blow up my world, professional and private.

"Indeed, it does. I feel closer to you than anyone else I've ever worked with or worked for in the past and present. It seems to me we're kindred spirits with regards to a lot of things, books, movies, and TV to name a few. I think it's possible that it could go deeper than just that."

As I read her words, they cocoon me in warmth. Is she saying what I think she's saying? Or is she just saying that we have a lot of things we like in common? Like we both eat eggs over easy and appreciate the words of JFK. My mind reels in confusion. Is she saying she wants a friendship with me or is she wanting more than that? Hoping it's more than that I start to type. "I agree with you I think it's more than just superficial things. I think it's more profound than that. I

18

might be overstepping right now. So please tell me of I am, and I'll drop it. As your friend, do you want to talk about things and maybe vent to me? How are you actually doing?"

After a heart pounding pause, I see Anne begin to type a reply back. "If I had to put things into words, I'd say I feel lonely and lost. I feel abandoned."

What I should feel is happy and hopeful because of what she's sent—I might actually have a chance. Instead, I feel a deep sadness from the words Anne has typed. Even though we're thousands of miles apart, how she feels wraps around me. I feel her hurt and want to pull her close into my arms and let her know she has someone who is there for her. I can't tell her how I feel right now. She's telling me how she feels; what do I say to something as deeply personal as this?

"Oh, Anne, I'm so sorry you're dealing with something like this. I can't say that I know exactly what you're experiencing right now. But I do know what feeling lost, lonely, and abandoned feels like. I can completely empathize with those emotions."

"I'm sorry I'm burdening you with all of this. It's a lot to drop on someone, especially when you don't know what's actually happening. I didn't mean to blind side you with all this heavy stuff. I'm sorry our conversation has turned into this. Especially at the time of night it is on your side."

"You didn't and aren't doing anything wrong. You're not burdening me with this. I said something and you replied honestly with your feelings. I see that as being a human being, and sometimes our real, deeply buried feelings just bubble to the surface. I know how that feels: you think you're okay and then suddenly, something strikes a chord inside and the next thing you know everything comes rushing out. I think everyone has felt this way before. I'm always here if you want to talk or vent."

"Thanks so much for being you. I'll keep everything you've said in mind. I'm starting to get hungry; I think I'm going to hop off for now. I'll see you in the morning."

"Goodnight, Anne. Remember, my virtual door is always open anytime of the day or night, and I know you have my number."

"Night, Helen."

Slumping back into my chair with a sigh, I start to think about everything that's transpired today. Immediately, I break out of my thoughts and pad into my kitchen with bare feet. I head straight to one of the cabinet doors. Opening the door, I pull out my bottle of ouzo, also known as ouzaki in Greece. On the shelf below, I snag two of the ouzo glasses setting there along with a rocks glass.

Heading over to the island I place everything down. I take the bottle and pour about a shot and a half into one of the ouzo glasses. Normally, I'd pour just a shot but after the day I've had, I settle on the shot and a half. I grab the two other glasses and turn around to face the refrigerator. With the other ouzo glass, I fill it three quarters of the way with cold filtered water from the in-door dispenser. I then fill the rocks glass with ice from the same dispenser. Turning back to the island, I set the glass filled with ice down.

Properly serving ouzo is somewhat of an artform. If you just add ice to ouzo without gradually cooling it down first, you'll get a film of anise oil crystals across the top of the glass. I take the water and slowly add enough until the ouzo turns a milky white color. I then add a couple of ice cubes to the milky beverage.

Grasping the ouzo in one hand, I finger grab the other two glasses with the other and head to my living room.

Setting everything on the end table (with coasters of course! No one likes rings on wooden tabletops) next to the couch, I flop down and inhale a deep holding breathe. I take a sip of my drink (ouzo is to be sipped never chugged); the taste of anise from the liquid warms my throat as I queue up the playlist I have for The Weeknd and let "Take My Breath" wash over me via the room's surround sound.

What in the living fuck just happened today? I went from having writer's block, to frantically trying to finish that damned report, to having a ton of bricks dropped on me via Anne's confession. My mind swirls as I sit there sipping and listening, head tossed against the back of the couch. I don't even know if I should be happy or sad over Anne's revelations. Adding more water to my drink I contemplate the situation. Anne thinks of me as a friend. She also confessed that she has a troubled marriage and feels all alone and lost to boot.

As much as I'd like for her to have romantic emotions about me, I know I can't ever broach that subject. It'd be wrong on so many levels, not to mention the fact that I'd never take advantage of someone in such a vulnerable state. I could never live with myself if I did that.

With a deep sigh, I take a sip and let the taste of anise roll through my mouth before warming my belly as I swallow. As my chest begins to relax from the tenseness of the day, I close my eyes and thoughts drift to Anne.

Imagining her being all alone at home. Seeing and feeling a sadness in her that's reflected in her eyes. Why does such a phenomenal person as her have to go through something like this? If Anne and I were together, I'd never take her for granted. I'd be cherishing every moment with her not being caught up in work.

As I continue to think about her, I notice that my right hand has worked its way down through the elastic waistline of my *The Bad Batch* lounge pants. Sipping my drink with my left hand I think about what it would be like to have Anne's lips again mine as my hand moves down closer to my core. Anne's lips grazing the bottom of my neck all the way to my jawline. Her lightly nipping at my lower lip with a smile playing across her slightly parted lips.

My fore and middle fingers begin to strum my drenched and glistening pearl in an alternating rhythm that is all my own. All the while I think of Anne being with me. Her cupping my face with both hands and deeply kissing me. Her sultry voice as she runs her hands all over my body, me in turn doing the same to her. Looking down I realize I've started to lightly thrust. Subconsciously touching my breasts and nipples, picturing Anne's hands and mouth as the instruments of my pleasure, as I hope I'd be the same for her.

As a moan escapes my lips, fantasy Anne of my dreams moves the party on down lower. I feel her tongue swirl my clit in circles of never-ending ecstasy. In my mind, I glance down and see her look up at me with a wicked grin and a glint to those gorgeous steel blue eyes. Another moan slips out as I smile down back at her just as stars erupt before my eyes. I toss my had back in euphoria and get lost in the moment.

Still panting, Anne and I move one hand to my slick entrance. Straddling me with one arm propped up and hovering over she enters me with two fingers. A gasp that I was holding in leaves my mouth as I eagerly envelope her fingers. Mirroring her I slip in two fingers of my own into her. I moan as I franticly thrust, lost in the moment, just picturing Anne over me, thrusting into me as I thrust into her in turn. Over and over as we both ride the wave to its crest where we are both left breathless and panting, longing for more.

After I come down, I get up and start to walk to my bedroom. Striping off my sweat and self-pleasured soaked clothes along the way. Letting them drop where they fall. I tumble into bed naked and alone thinking of the Anne I'll never have beside me to warm me on cold nights like these as I drift off to slept.

Chapter Three

I WAS PEACEFULLY SLEEPING; now, I'm not. Now, I'm listening to the piercing sound of the klaxon alarm going off on my phone, startling me awake. It's the only sound that'll wake me up; I've been known to sleep through tornado sirens, but that's a story for another time. I'm so not a morning person so I only give myself thirty minutes to get ready before work. That means during the work week I need to hit the ground running, otherwise I'd play snooze button roulette until the cows come home. With this in mind, I hit the off button on my alarm and swing my legs out of bed and get moving.

First, I let the girls outside for a quick pee break. While that's happening, I'm getting food in their bowls and coffee going. Once that's done, I'm getting them both inside. Under the warm water of the shower, I'm still trying to shake off everything that happened yesterday. By the time I'm done and dressed and in front of my laptop, I think I'm clear headed. Or at least, I hope I am. I have another busy day ahead of me and on top of that, it's Friday.

The day passes by quickly and uneventfully, thankfully

everything that happened the day before not even crossing my mind because I've been so busy with my work and escalations to even have darned to even entertain the thought. Since it's six pm my time, I start to think about getting some writing in. I open my manuscript file and reread what I've typed.

My tormentor burps with a sound like a hyena, having eaten the last of the food.

Okay I can work with this. It's not great but it's also not terrible. Now what the heck do I write as a follow up line?

He sits there with a container of fried chicken, munching away on his food and drool.

Okay, I like that. There might be a story in this. I might not be a failure after all. Maybe Anne is right. And just like that, all my thoughts return to her, my muse, the woman that believes in me. The one that I can't let myself fall in love with for a host of reasons. I cast Ava Max's music from my phone over to my office speakers and try to buckle down and get back to writing.

"You know, I haven't eaten all day," the teenage girl says.

"I don't care. You're just an eventual paycheck," the one known as Lossif, one of my tormentors, replies.

My name is Rachil, and I'm fifteen years old. I was kidnapped on my way home from school, on what I now think was two days ago. It might be three days ago. I'm in a windowless room, so it's hard to tell how much time has passed. I think I was kidnapped because my father is somehow involved with some drug cartel. My dad thinks my mom and I don't know, but we do, we just don't talk about it. Weird people show up at our door at odd hours of the day and night. I wish we had been told about Dad's involvement because then I might have known what to do in a situation like this. Instead, here I sit on a wobbly wooden chair, at an old worn table, watching this guy stuff his face with the only food in the nearest vicinity.

Well, that felt good to get something out onto virtual paper. What didn't feel good was as usual I didn't write a story outline which is manuscript writing 101. I've never been able to do one. It isn't how my brain is wired, and it kills me every time I need to write a story because I never have a plan and this time it's no different. So again, I was shooting from the hip. At least this time I felt like I was off to somewhat of a good start. Only time will tell for sure.

My stomach rumbling is my que that it might be time to think about doing something about dinner. Getting up, I do a mental inventory of what I might have on hand that could be quick and easy, the two keywords that are my go to's with regards to eating. I settle on a bowl of Froot Loops. Before I take care of myself, I make sure to feed Eleni and Georgie, not that the girls would ever let me forget about them. Girls done, I pour some cereal with cold milk into a bowl. I grab a teaspoon on my way out into the living room.

I grab the TV remote and settle into one of my leather reclining loveseats. I pull up the episode of *The Expanse* that I'm behind on and begin to watch while eating dinner surrounded by two dogs hoping that I'll miss my mouth so they can grab some Froot Loops, too.

After the episode is over—which by the way my team was right, it was really good—I check my phone and I'm greeted with some texts from various friends. Some who want me to go hang out at their houses with them and some others who want to go out and do something. After replying no kindly to them all I go back to the TV remote and also pull up my TV show tracker app on my phone to see what other shows I'm behind on.

This week has left me wanting nothing more than to curl up on my couch with some childhood sugary cereal, my dogs, a warm throw, and the TV. Looking at the app on my phone I see *Star Wars: The Bad Batch* is next on my list of things to watch. *The Bad Batch* is one of my favorite shows. It's also one of Anne's favorite shows as well. And there it is again. I'm right back to Anne. When I should be decompressing and thinking about me. I banish all thoughts of her from my mind and pull up the current season and the oldest episode I haven't seen yet.

Just as I'm finishing the last episode, including fast forwarding through all the credits just to make sure there aren't any extra scenes at the end of it, I hear the Slack app on my phone ding. With dread I pick up my phone and glance at it, hoping it's not Rhett bugging me with some outlandish idea. I know I'm salary, but it's the start of the weekend, and I'd like to have one. It turns out it's not Rhett; it's Anne. I don't know what's worse for me right now.

The message reads, "I feel my ears burning. Did a certain someone watch a certain something?"

"As they should. I'm sitting in my living room, and I've just finished getting caught up on *The Expanse* and *The Bad Batch*."

"That *Expanse* episode was so good, right?"

I know there has to be something up on her side for her to reach out to me on a Friday night. I'm not sure whether to broach the subject yet or not. I'm going to try and feel things out with her first.

"It sure was! You guys were so right. I can't wait to talk about it with everyone during our next team meeting."

"Christos and Davitt and going to be so jazzed about that next week, I'm sure. What did you think of *The Bad Batch* episode? How far behind were you? Was it just one or was it two?"

"It was two and great as always, and as predicted, Omega stole the show, as she should."

"She really is great, isn't she?"

"She really is."

"And how's the writing coming along?"

Still nothing but small talk from her.

"I got some words down on a page, so that's something. I'm feeling better about things. I kind of have an outline going on in my head about things this time. What I do know is that next time, I'm definitely doing an outline come the next book. I can't continue limping along like this any longer."

"Don't beat yourself up over it. I was completely the same way in the beginning when I first started writing. I never wanted to plot plan anything out. I wanted everything to be fresh, right from my mind and direct from there to the keyboard."

Still always my champion and in my corner encouraging me.

"Exactly! If I try and formulize it, then it's gonna sound all dead and canned. Not fresh and new like I want it to."

"Trust me, you can still plan and have it still sounds fresh and new."

I can't wait any longer; I need to check in on her and find out what's going on.

"Okay, Sensei, I believe you. Now, aside from feeling your ears burning, what's up tonight?"

I see the three dots that signify that Anne's been typing hang there for a bit.

Finally, I see words spill across the screen of my phone from Anne.

"Jose and I had another fight. He told me earlier that after he finishes with work he's going out and that I shouldn't wait up for him."

"Well, ain't that some heavy shit to be greeted with on a Friday. I'm so damn sorry you're dealing with a load of crap like that. Have a fight with someone, fine. But don't leave a person hanging like that, especially someone whom you supposedly love," I type without even thinking.

"Shit," I type right away and hit enter.

"It's not my place to have said that." I hit enter again.

"Please forgive my off the cuff remakes." Enter.

"I was completely out of line." Enter.

"I should never have said any of that." Enter.

"You're not wrong," Anne replies back.

I am stunned.

"Everything you've just said is right," she says.

I am shocked.

"If he loved me, he wouldn't treat me like shit," Anne types.

"If he cared about me, he would love me," Anne sends.

"If he wanted me, he'd be coming home. Not staying out doing god knows what," Anne says.

"Do you just want to call me? It might be easier than typing at this point? That is if you're up to it." I see my fingers ghost typing of their own volition. It's like I'm having an out of body experience right now.

What the fuck am I doing right now?

I must be insane

Did I somehow hit my head and just not realize it?

It's Anne. She'd do the same for you, you ass.

I get up, taking my phone and empty bowl with me and head for the wine fridge in the kitchen. Just as I'm placing the bowl in the sink, my phone begins to ring. I answer it without looking and place it on speaker.

"Hello there," I say as I pull out a wine glass etched with a lightsaber out of one of the cabinets.

"I hope I didn't catch you at a bad time," I hear Anne's smoky voice come through the speaker. She's trying to sound upbeat, but I can tell she's sad.

"No, you've called just in time for dessert," I say as I head to the wine fridge and pull out a bottle of Barefoot Sweet Red Blend.

"Earlier, it was Froot Loops for dinner," I continue as I twist the cap off the ten-dollar bottle of wine and pour a glass. Then take the bottle with the glass and head back into the living room. "Now, it's a glass of Sweet Red Blend by Barefoot. One of my absolute favorites."

"I'm glad I have impeccable timing then," she says with a slight giggle.

Returning to the living room, I set everything down on the side table. I slump back down onto the couch and with a heavy sigh I say, "Anne, talk to me. What's going on? What happened today? Are you okay?"

There is a pause followed by a deep breath which I can hear though the phone. After that I can feel a deep sigh chased by a swallow.

"Yeah, I think so," is the slow response I get back from her.

"I'll take that." I drink a long sip of wine.

I hear rummaging and what sounds like a glass being set down on something. Next, I hear something being unscrewed.

"Can't have you drinking alone," she says as I hear liquid pouring into a glass.

"What's your poison tonight?" I ask.

"Coincidentally, the same as yours, Sweet Red Blend

by Barefoot. Great minds. I guess another thing we have in common, a love of sweet red wines."

"But is it in a lightsaber wine glass?"

"No, only a *may the force be with you* one," she says.

"Close enough," I reply.

"Good wine may only be drunk in *Star Wars* wine glasses." I hear her take a long drink and swallow.

"Damn straight." I pause, biting my tongue. "Anne, are you really okay?"

"No"

"Do you want to talk about it?"

"Yes." I hear her sigh. "Where do I start? Maybe the beginning? I guess that's where I'd like to start."

"Sounds like a good spot to me," I reply.

"We've been together for six years. Of that we've been married for five of those years. The first year we were dating I thought things were fine but when I look back upon our early relationship now, I realize things weren't fine. In the beginning, he would say he'd like to read and walk trails or go to the beach. All things I really enjoy doing." I hear the tiredness in her voice.

"You do really like those things, just like I do," I replied.

"You know me. I like to read a book and talk about it. That's so not Jose. Nor is taking a walk along a trail or even our neighborhood. Let alone the beach," she says with a tinge of sadness.

"You for sure love doing those things," I say.

"Another thing would be that I really like to go to amusement parks. He'd say that he'd like to go to those, too. So, in the beginning, we'd do all of those things and he'd act like he actually liked doing all of those things. But as our relationship grew through the years, he'd show less and less interest in those things and more attention toward things he'd want to do."

"That's really not fair to you. A relationship is, as you know, all about give and take. So, you weren't doing anything wrong," I tell her, trying to sound comforting.

God, this guy sounds like an ass, for sure.

"Thanks for saying that, Helen. So, because I was in love with him, I'd show genuine interest in learning about his hobbies and interests and actually grew to like some of them, too."

Was in love with him? I hate myself for focusing on this the most of everything Anne has just said, but that's what I hear the hardest. There's conviction in her voice. She really has given *everything*. And she's no longer in love with this man.

Which means there could be something between us.

Stop! I tell myself. Don't even go there. Especially not now.

"Like for instance, arena football," Anne says. "Once I understood it, I fell in love with the game and really enjoyed going to games with him. Wrestling was another thing I learned about from him and really enjoyed watching at home or going to an event in person with him."

"It's truly amazing that you were able to embrace some of his interests and hobbies and share them with him. And he wasn't able to turnaround and even try and do the same for you at all. Did he even try to?" I asked.

"Repeatedly, if I look back, there were signs. I think he was faking his enthusiasm all along. I knew there were red flags, but he was such a nice guy overall and he never really was a bad guy." There's exasperation in her voice.

"I get it. Sometimes things seem different then they are at the time," I say, taking a deep sip of wine. *What am*

I doing? I think I may have bitten off more than I can chew.

"They were, and they weren't. After a while, he'd grumble and roll his eyes if I'd bring up just simply going for a walk. Or if I'd want to book a trip somewhere he'd say, 'Why go somewhere when we could just watch it on TV?'"

"Damn. I'd say, yeah, that's definitely some signs right there."

"I think I ended up marrying him because he was nice enough and never mean to me. I'd been through some abusive relationships before Jose, so back then, nice seemed perfect. Only through time did I learn that there's more to a healthy relationship than kindness."

Abusive relationships? My heart hurts for Anne, gut twisting in knots. Who the hell would mistreat such a kind person? I want to ask Anne who these people are, so I can give them a piece of my mind, but I stop for obvious reasons. That would be bad on all accounts.

"In the end, we were never right for each other," Anne continues. "Even on my wedding day, I thought if it wasn't right, I'd have cold feet, and I didn't. So even that's a misnomer. I also think I was at a different place in my life than I am today."

Her final sentiment ends on a more analytical tone. As if she's thinking about things as she says them out loud.

With a deep breath, Anne says, "So, that's the short and skinny of my relationship with Jose."

"And quite the relationship it is." I chuckle uncomfortably, still reeling from everything she's shared with me. Do I even *dare* to go *there*? Those dark times that I've bottled up and hidden away so they never see the light of day. Cast away so that I'm never subjected to that menagerie of pain (mental and emotional) and the humiliation and embarrassment again. I've not at any time told a soul what I've been through *ever*. Was now the time? I take a deep sip of wine and draw a cleansing breath.

"Anne, I'm going to tell you some things about myself that no one at work knows. Even my friends don't know because I hid it all from them at the time. I was in several abusive relationships when I was younger. So, I understand your pain and why you'd pick a nice man and settle."

"Really?"

"Really. The first time it was a high school boyfriend; I was just fifteen. In the beginning, Jim was really nice but as things progressed, he became very possessive of me. He had to know where I was and who I was with at all times. In the end he was emotionally and physically abusive. My parents found out and got the police involved, which come to think of it was kind of unheard of back then."

"Wow, I could never picture that happening to someone like you."

"Someone like me? I'm not following?"

"I mean, to someone so self-assured and confident."

"Abuse happens to all sorts of people, from all walks of life."

"Oh, of course. I guess it's just hard for me hearing that you experienced all this, too, and it makes my heart heavy."

I pause and take another deep breath. Can I share this next story with her? This one touches on my sexual orientation. Another thing no one at work knows about because I don't discuss it. Period.

"I'm going to share another story, but this one is even more sensitive and personal to me, because it concerns my sexual orientation," I say. "I'm bisexual and I'm very private with that. The abuse was committed by a woman, so I thought I was safe at the time, until I wasn't. This woman was also my professor at college."

"That's awful! It sounds like she took advantage of you," Anne says. "Also, so we're on the same page, your private life is your own, just as I know mine is safe with you."

"Thank you for saying that. Anne, your past and present is safe with me." I take another deep, calming breath. "Where was I? Oh, yes, now I remember. I was a sophomore in college. I was taking a forensics anthropology course. My professor's name was Garnet, and she was twenty years my senior. At first it was exhilarating, we had so many things in common and I had so many things to learn from her. She was writing a novel on the side about a forensic anthropologist who was solving crimes. She called me her muse and used to flatter me all the time."

"That had to have been exciting for someone at that age."

"It really was. Then, she started using me. First it was my credit cards to pay for things. She'd say things like all her money was tied up in her writing with cover art, editing, cost of living and that being a professor didn't actually pay much. Then, it was mental. Garnet would call me an idiot or say I was stupid or not old enough to understand something. It might also be that I didn't have the life experience to know something even though I knew I did."

"Boy, have I heard all of that before."

"I heard, 'You're just a kid' or she'd call me a baby more times than I care to remember. It culminated into physical abuse. First, she'd grab me by the arm kind of hard. Then it would be hard enough to leave a bruise. Next, it would be by the hair. After that, it would be slaps across the face, well enough to see a hand imprint. I feared for my life on more than one occasion. When I tried covering up the blackeyes and bruised ribs, my friends noticed. They threatened to go to the dean if I didn't break it off with her. I finally did after more than a year of being with her with their help."

"How did you come back from something like that?"

"I didn't at first. I felt stupid and ashamed. I felt swindled and abused. Internally, I curled up into a ball. Externally, it was business as usual, everyone was none the wiser. Inside, I was utter turmoil, nothing but chaos. I was broken and shattered.

"I figured I would be safe trusting someone older than me because we're raised to trust our elders. I thought I was doubly safe trusting a woman because women are, well, nurturing by nature, or so I assumed. I was I so wrong on both accounts. Women can be as unhealthy as men, because women are people, too.

"What I did learn in the end is that you cannot let bad experiences color your whole view on life. I did eventually heal and did get myself back out there and went on to date some very wonderful people, both men and women.

"I will also say that when I did start dating again the first person after Garnet was not right for me. She was very sweet, but she wasn't the right person for me, and we both knew that. We really didn't have anything in common, but that relationship gave me the opportunity to heal. Which in the end, I was very grateful for.

"Anne, you're the first person to ever hear both of those stories. And as I'm sure you know, my whole point in telling you is, you're not alone. Abuse happens and can happen to the ones we know, including me."

I clear my head and collect my thoughts as I pour another glass of wine. I think I did the right thing by telling her my story. I'm always nervous with sharing deep private parts of myself with others. Especially someone like Anne whom I have strong colored feelings for.

"Until now," she says, "I would have never known you had been in several abusive relationships."

"I could say the same about you. I see you as caring, strong, and confident."

"You do?"

"I do. Anne, you're extraordinary."

"No, that's you."

"No, I'm a dork. I'm envious of all your talents."

"What talents?"

"Ugh, don't get me started. You can write, you can program, you project manage, you can draw, you can sing —yes, I caught the tail end of you singing with the guys on a video meeting one time. Oh, where was I? You're good at any random thing I ask you to do. Whenever I have a plot hole, you know how to fill it right away."

"I am none of those things!"

"Yes, you are! Even your hair is perfect! Just like your eyes! Shit did I say that out loud? Shit, I did, didn't I? Ugh. I'm gonna crawl under a rock now."

Christ, what did I just do? She's hurting and in pain.

"Helen! Come back now! I like your eyes more than mine."

Wait! What? She does?

"Wait? You do? What? Mine are shit brown. Yours are the most unique steel blue that I've ever seen, they're all your own. I've never seen eyes like yours, *ever*."

What am I doing right now? *I need to stop! Now!*

"And yours are a most unique chestnut brown that are all your own, that *I've* never seen before," Anne says. "And since we're going there, your hair is better than mine."

"Is not. Mine is pulled up all the time for a reason."

"And I don't care, I like it."

37

"I guess I just need to stop and take the compliment. Thank you for saying all of that."

"And thank you for saying everything you've said about me. And I guess if I'm being honest, I haven't had someone compliment me in a pretty long time. It feels nice."

I'm worried she's not okay with everything I've just blurted out, coupled along with me being bi. I need to find out.

"Same here. I feel embarrassed, but it does feel good. I also hope I didn't make you feel uncomfortable by just blurting things out. I didn't mean to say the things I said, they just came tumbling out. I also don't want to you to feel uncomfortable because of my sexual orientation. Please be honest if either of them does. I need to know."

"Oh, heck no! And I think if we're both being truthful with ourselves, we've both felt something between us. I feel like we've been dancing around it. I've even tried dropping some hints with you."

Oh! My! God! She *has* been flirting with me after all! I *was* right! I wasn't reading into anything.

"So, you were flirting with me! I was never one hundred percent sure, so I always just let it be. Yes, I always felt like there was some chemistry there between us. I just never did anything about it for all the obvious reasons."

"I get it and totally understand. We work together. You're my boss. Plus, you knew I was married, you just didn't know I wasn't happily married."

"Yup, all of the things you listed above. Anne, can I back up and ask you some questions about some various stuff?"

I think my head just exploded again for a bunch of reasons. I need to get answers and now.

"Sure. Anything. Shoot away."

Jose. What's *actually* happening with him.

"What are you planning to do about what's going on with Jose?" I ask.

"I've asked him for a divorce on a few occasions now. He never answers me back. I think he knows we should deep down inside, but he doesn't want to face the truth because he'd see that as a failure. I'd say couples therapy but like I've said before we're just not right for each other."

Man is this guy a super putz.

"But marriages don't work out every day," I say. "It happens."

"I know that, and you know that. He just doesn't see it that way."

"Sounds majorly frustrating."

"Sigh. Trust me, it is. What's your next question?"

Here's the bigger question I need the answer to.

"Have you ever had feelings for a woman before?"

"Oh, that's an easy one. Yes, a few times in fact, but they've only ever been crushes that I'd never pursued. I'd wanted to but I was too shy and nervous to do anything about them. In addition, I wasn't sure if the person shared the same feelings as me or was the same orientation. As you know the world can be a minefield in that regard."

"Oh, god, do I know. I don't feel the need to broadcast my orientation via hairstyles or dress, but I also don't feel the need to hide it if that makes any sense. I'm just me."

"Exactly! At this point, I feel like there should be some sort of secret handshake or something."

"I agree, it would just make it all so much easier."

While this revelation about Anne's feelings makes my heart leap for joy, a heavy reminder of work slaps me in the face.

"Anne."

"Yes, Helen?"

"This really can't go beyond harmless flirtation for the reasons we've discussed."

"I know. As much as I want it to."

"I'll be honest, I wish things were different, but they're not."

"This has nothing to do with you, but I really need to sit down with Jose and spell things out to him. I also need to start calling around to find an attorney to get the ball rolling on that front. I owe it to him and myself."

"Please let me know if you need any help with that. Our company has resources that are available to you free of charge. I'll email the links over to you. Also, as you know, I'm a phone call away."

"Thanks for letting me know about the services; I just might need them. As always thanks for always being supportive of me."

"Hey, you're just as supportive of me as I am of you. Don't forget that. I'm glad we've cleared the air about our feelings. And I'm glad you felt that you could trust me enough to talk to me about what's been going on at home with Jose."

"You were the one who was trusting enough to talk about the abuse from your past. That took a ton of courage right there. Helen, you are so damn strong. I'm proud to call you my friend. Then on top of that, you trusted me enough to discuss your orientation. Not many people would take that chance, but you saw that I needed to hear someone else's abuse story. I will never forget what you shared with me."

"I knew that I could trust you since you trusted me. Again, we both know we have this connection between us. It's like we've known each other since forever."

"True."

I look down at my phone. Shit, is it really that late?

"It's like three forty-five my time so that's like what your time? Twelve forty-five, right?"

"Oh, my goodness, it is. I just looked down at my phone. I'm so sorry I kept you up this late."

"No, no, it's fine we were both talking to each other. We can talk more on Monday. I know it's going to be hard with everything going on but please try and get some rest over the weekend. And if you need time-off just let me know."

"I'm going to try to. Please do the same. I know it's been a long week and a long night. See you on Monday. Night, Helen."

"Night, Anne."

Neither one of us hangs up.

"One of us has to hang up," I say.

"I was waiting for you," Anne replies.

We both giggle.

"On the count of three," I say. "One, two, three."

We both hang up.

I slump back into the couch.

She was flirting with me.

She likes me.

We both like each other.

Nothing can come of this.

She's married.

Unhappily, I remind myself.

Still married.

She's three thousand miles away.

So what.

She works for you.

There's a work policy against it.

So, I switch teams.

How do you know it'll work out?

I don't.

I'm putting the cart before the horse.

Getting up I go to my room, stripping off my clothes as I enter and crawl under the comforter. No sooner have I shut my eyes then I drift off to sleep with thoughts of Anne in my dreams.

Chapter Four

Squeezing my eyes shut tighter isn't helping. I still hear panting, and I'm still being slapped in the face by a Pomeranian. One specifically named Eleni. Peeling one eye open I steal a glance at my watch between well landed precision slaps. It's nine am already so that explains it. With a groan I toss my legs over the side of the bed and get up and head to the kitchen. First, I let the kids outside via the sliders. One issue down, one more to go. Next, I pour some food into their bowls.

Now I get a cup of coffee going for myself. Breakfast for today is going to be blueberry yogurt with some granola. Coffee fixed with cream and sugar and in hand, I let the girls back in to eat. I settle down to eat as well as I read the morning news on my phone. After eating, the small number of dishes are loaded into the dishwasher.

I realize I'm thinking about everything that happened last night. I need to clear my thoughts, I head for the basement and my rowing machine. First things first though, before I can even think about sweating anything out, let alone working anything out in my head, I need to find some good music that fits my mood. I think for a second and settle on some Duran Duran and start out with "New Moon on Monday."

Music settled on, I ease into rowing, slowly at first. I pull on the cable with my eyes closed and listen to the music and the whirl of the cable and the wheel of the rowing machine. I feel the seat slide along the rail and soon I'm just lost in the motion of everything working together, myself included. The music is pumping, my muscles are working, the wheel is whirling, the seat is sliding along the rail. Everything is all one big orchestra working in time together. There is no me, no Anne, no work, no anything.

I stop once my arms and legs are jelly, which is about an hour. I head back upstairs for a well-deserved shower. I step under the warm water coming out of the rain shower-head. One of the best investments I've made to the master bath of the house. I lean against the wall with my hands and bow my head to allow the water wash over me and let the warmth work into my tired muscles.

My mind wanders as I'm under the water. I think about Anne even though I shouldn't be. I picture her messaging the calming body wash into my shoulders. Damn does that feel so good. It feels even better as she moves down my body, lathering me up as she goes. I turn to her and do the same. Paying extra attention to her exquisite breasts as I let myself get lost in her electrifying eyes.

I rinse my hand and start to massage her bundle of nerves with my index finger, I feel her arch her back and move closer into me as I do this. Moving lower I enter her with two fingers and feel her lightly bite my shoulder as I begin to rock in and out of her. I gasp in surprise and plea-sure at the mild pain of the love bite.

44

Suddenly, I'm pleasantly greeted with fingers entering me as well. We both grasp on to one another and rock in and out of each other in unison. Our breathes quicken as we race closer and closer to our shared release. Kisses become more frantic in-between uncontrollable moans escaping from our lips. The pace accelerates to a dizzying speed until stars explode in front of our eyes and we're left panting and holding on to each other.

When my vision clears, I realize I'm holding the shower wand and it's pointed at my core. Once the water has done its job, I finish up and get on with the rest of my morning.

* * *

With the dishwasher loaded up and running, I toss the damp tea towel onto the freshly cleaned counter. I hear the Roomba off in the distance terrorizing the children. The last of the laundry has been folded and put away. Check, check, and check. The last thing left on my list is grocery shopping. Do I brave the actual store or do I Instacart it all? Decisions, decisions. On the one hand, it would be nice to get and have some time outside of the house.

What folks don't seem to get about working from home full-time is that if you don't watch yourself, you can quickly become a hermit. I choose to go with ye ole Instacart this time with the internal promise to myself that I'll venture out into the public eye next food order. I quickly create an order for the week. With that done, I head to my office to write.

Writing has never been an easy thing for me to do. It's always been a struggle and I always find every excuse in the book to not do it. Having a deadline really helps with that. Anne helps with that. And just like that, I'm back to thinking about her, when I should be focusing on this story that I need to so desperately make some headway with. I bury my head down in my laptop and start to type.

"I'm sure my parents haven't even noticed I've been gone. I wonder *if the school has called? Like I said earlier, my dad, Dimitrios, is an accountant for some sort of drug cartel. He's a hard-working guy who loves his family but never has time for us. He's so busy I'm sure he hasn't noticed my absence. My mom, Priscillia, is so self-absorbed I'm confident she hasn't and just wouldn't care, because she's all about her and only her. I'm not even sure why my dad married her.*

There is definitely one person in this world who has noticed that I'm literally missing. And whom is that might you ask? That would be the love of my life and my soulmate. She knows that something is greatly wrong. Jamie is seventeen and we both live for each other. We met when I was thirteen; it was truly love at first sight that day at the mall. We were both walking into Gamestop at the exact same time and bumped into each other. Then, throughout our whole time there, we kept going down the same isles. It was pretty funny and even more funny if you were actually there.

Here's the problem: have these idiots even asked for a ransom yet? What are my parents doing about my situation? I think I have a way of communicating with Jamie, but I don't want to do anything unless I have more info. Also, I've told Jamie about what my dad does, but I haven't told my family that I've told Jamie. So, yeah, super awkward if I send her over there to say, 'Yeah, I know your daughter has been kidnapped because she's contacted me to ask you guys what's going on with it.'

Where I'm being kept appears to be some sort of studio apartment with the main room divided by a low wall. The living area where there's a TV with a couch with recliner along with a single bed in a corner with a bathroom off through another door. The kitchen area has a small dining table with a hotplate and a fridge.

Currently, I'm laying on the bed facing the wall. They've taken my iPhone but not my Apple Watch which has cellular built into it, so I don't need my phone to use it for data. I slyly pull my apple watch up to my face and begin to quietly type a message to Jamie.

> Luv been kidnapped 4 ransom not sure rents know. Dads jobs might not have told him. They might not send hlp Not sure what to do. Im scared not sure where am. Txting wit watch. Need hlp

Thankfully, I always have my watch and phone on silent, so these goobers won't know I've been using it. After a minute or so I get a reply.

> Rachil Ive been sick 2 death worrying about u since I haven't heard from u in a couple of days which isn't normal for u. I agree dads job probably isnt coming. I have some friends who should be able 2 hlp. I need u 2 tell me when & how were u grabbed & how long did it take them to bring u 2 where u @ what does place look like

I think back to the moments before my abduction. I had just stepped outside of school and was walking across the street to meetup with Jamie and a group of friends up at a coffee shop a block or so away when a black commercial delivery van came screaming up beside me.

A side door slid open and a set of burly arms shot out and snatched me inside. Where I had a sack that smelled like garlic tossed over my head. The van had been heading north when it had grabbed me and had taken a hard right at the first corner which would have been at the corner of my school's campus.

47

After that it had stayed on the same street for about five minutes where it took another right. After another ten minutes it took a left and after five minutes it stopped into front of the building, I was now in. When I was dragged out, I could smell sea spray and hear ship horns in the distance.

I type all of this to Jamie and right away I got back.

> Luv, all of those deets are great. Im going 2 talk 2 some friends I know ttys my luv

I immediately type back:

> I luv u so much my everything

I hit save on the document even though I have the software set to automatically save it. My story started out as something different, but I'm pleased with the change of events. Standing, I take a long deep stretch, arching my back, which works the kinks out of it.

Still feeling out of sorts with the events of the past couple of days, I head back to the basement. It's there that I pull out one of my thicker yoga mats. Sitting down on it, I pipe some sound bath music from my phone through the speakers down there. I close my eyes and work on entering a meditative state for twenty minutes or so, just enough time to allow myself to recenter and reground.

After that the rest of the day passes uneventfully until it's time for bed. This time I allow myself time for a couple of relaxing yoga positions before tucking myself into bed with some mint tea, a *Star Wars* novel, and two little dogs. I read for about an hour before turning off the lights. Try though as I might, thoughts of Anne enter my sleeping moments. I see her beautiful smile and hear her musical voice in my dreams. Though I sleep I do not truly rest because Anne is everywhere. I don't know if this is good or bad or if it's the universe sending me a message or even what the heck it is.

Chapter Five

It's been a busy couple days at work since this past weekend. Today is my weekly one on one meeting with Anne. I'm not going to lie, I'm a bit nervous about it with everything that's gone down recently. How different is our dynamic going to be now? Is everything going to be super awkward or really weird? I've been worried about it all day.

I think all these thoughts while tilting my head one way and then another as I look at a map of California. Clicking on various towns along the coast. As much as I like the cool weather, this time I think my soul calls for the warm salt air and not the coolness of the mountains and snowiness of the slops. I don't want to be too far south where it gets too hot. God, do I hate the heat, even with a coastal breeze.

Minimizing the window quickly I reach for my phone and open my personal calendar and make a note to reach out to an old associate about something that's been on my mind before I forget about it. I then get back to work reviewing various metrics before I need to wrap them up into a report later on in the week. It's getting to be later on in the day for me, so brain fog has started to set in. I'm having the damnedest time with focusing on these metrics. Not to mention, I still have Anne first and foremost on my mind.

* * *

I'm two minutes early and Anne's already in the video call for our meeting. I'm nervous about how this is going to go, but I'm hopeful it's just business as usual. I bite the bullet, hope for the best, and hit the join button.

"Anne, how goes it?"

"Hi, Helen, it goes!"

"For reals, I hope works hasn't been too crazy for you!"

"It hasn't, and I hope it hasn't been for you either!'

"Just the same reporting hell stuff it all. No bigs at all."

"That's good."

"Now truthfully, is there anything I can help you with? Anyone who's giving you pushback on any of your projects or anything?"

"Nah, I got it all under control."

"Christos?"

"Honestly, he's been getting better."

God, those eyes.

"That's good to hear."

"Yeah, it's like he's had an about face or something."

I hear and see Anne giggle knowingly.

And that giggle and smile. I really need to let this go. This will cost me my job if I'm not careful.

"You have anything to do with that?" she asks.

I hear the playfulness in her voice and see it in her eyes.

She knows full well I can't comment on that. I had a come to Jesus talk with him on Monday. After Davit came to me in frustration yet again. I knew enough was enough and that Anne was too nice to ever come to me.

"You know full well I can't say either way," I say with a twinkle in my eye.

"Oh, my god! thank you so much!"

"Moving on, anything else?" as I try and hide a smirk

"About the other night," she begins to say.

Holding up a hand, I gently cut her off. We can't go there. Not now. Against my better judgement, I point to my phone and quickly text her that it's not a good idea to talk about personal things on company equipment and over company accounts. As if my fingers are ghostwriting for me yet again, I then text her my personal email address and tell her we can video chat later over that account.

Anne nods in understanding, and I quickly get a reply from her with her personal email account info as well.

"Unless you have anything else for me, I'll give you back some of your time."

"No, I think I'm good."

We both click off.

I let out a deep breath that I didn't even realize I was holding.

It wasn't as awkward as I thought it was going to be, but it was awkward enough. It was still uncomfortable though. I need to do something about this.

I clear my head and get back to closing out my workday by clearing my email inbox. I swear emails multiply on their own. I hear my work chat ping. A quick glance shows me it's Davit with a quick question about a project he's working on.

"Hi, Davit!"

"Hey, Boss! Sorry to bother you so late but for any software bugs found on this project who do I direct them to?"

"Off the top of my head, I think it's Saul Goodman. If it's not him, he'll know who's handling them."

"Thanks again. Have a good one."

"Same to you."

I really do like my team. It would be a very hard choice for me to make if I ever did decide to leave.

* * *

Pacing back and forth on my deck looking out at the water, I wage an inner war with myself. Do I reach out to Anne, or do I wait for her to reach out to me? Or do I do the right thing and just let the whole thing go and let sleeping dogs lie, so to speak, as I should? I'm drawn to her like a moth to a flame. I definitely know better, but with the revelation that she also likes me, well, that's for sure ground changing. But again, she has some housekeeping to do on her end to even think about even beginning something, and is this worth me losing or giving up my job on just a whim or a hint of something? I know deep down my feelings and desires are none of those, my emotions run far more powerful than that.

I'm left even more confused than when I started. I stop pacing and just stop and stare out at the lapping waves willing them to have all the answers that I desperately need. Whistling down to Eleni and Georgie playing down in the yard to come in. I wait for them to come back on the deck. Then, the three of us step back inside. I know what I need to do next; butterflies stir throughout my body at the thought of it.

Glancing down at my watch, I make sure it's past eight pm my time, which it is. In fact, it's eight fifteen. She should be done with work, if not close to it. Looking around, I see my phone on the counter and snatch it up and shoot her a text asking her if she's free for an outside of work video chat. I soon get a reply of yes, so I grab my iPad and send over the invite and settle into one of the living room loveseats and wait for her to join. Soon I hear her doing just that.

I try to not let my nerves get the best of me as I greet her.

"Hi!" I say

"Well, hello there,"

There's that voice of hers, it hits me right down in my core. I feel myself start to throb. This goes beyond sexual attraction. Oh, that's there, too. But there's also something more about her that calls to my soul and makes it sing.

"I just wanted to let you talk about what you'd brought up earlier today over a safe avenue," I say. "Then we can go from there. Do you have the time for that? And are you able to talk?"

"Yeah, Jose is going to be working late again."

"So, I guess he eventually did end up coming home?"

"He came rolling in at about three that same night reeking of booze, cigarettes, and cheap perfume."

He has the most amazing woman at home, but from the description, it sounds like he was off at some strip club. If we were together, I'd *never* do that to her. I'd never *want* to do that to her. I'd want to be with her every moment that I could. I'd want to cherish her. *Stop going there, right now!*

"Was that upsetting to you?" I ask.

"Honestly, no, I hope he's finding a life outside of me. I've been ready to move on as you know for a long time now."

"I hope you're both able to amicability work things out so it's not such a blow for him, so things are easier for your side."

"I'm crossing my fingers but not holding my breath."

"That is a total mood and perspective."

"It sure is."

"So, what about the other night did you want to talk to me about?"

I absent mindedly remove the hair tie holding my hair up and let my hair down as we talk.

She sheepishly smiles at me. Damn her smile gets me every time.

"First off, thank you for telling me your story. That takes a ton of courage to talk about the things you spoke about."

"You needed to hear that you weren't alone in the world. That there are others out there that have had your same exact experiences. I did what needed to be done, that's all."

"I've been thinking about everything we talked about on Friday night and how nothing can come of it. Helen, how can we stop when we've started to become so friendly with each other?"

I was afraid she was going to bring something like this up. This sooo isn't helping my resolve in the least.

"We can still remain friendly at work. That doesn't have to change. We can probably also have a friendship outside of work as well, but anything else is a slippery slope. I for one know I like and need my job, and I'm pretty sure you feel the same way. Don't you?"

I watch her nod and say, "I do, but I still feel this deep connection between us..."

"I feel it, too, but we can't give into it; there's too much at stake. Anne, I have a mortgage and bills to pay and so do you."

"You're right. You are absolutely right. It's just so hard

and there's the what ifs at the back of my mind wanting to know. The,n there's regrets of not knowing."

"If this gets out and we're fired, word will get out to other tech companies. It will be difficult to get another job. This is how this works. Trust me. I've seen it before. I've seen it happen to former coworkers."

"We also don't know anything we live on different coasts. What harm are we causing anyone by just talking to each other? As far as I know, you're single, am I right?"

"You're right, I am, but you're not."

"As I've told you, my marriage has been over for years. So, you're not making anything worse there. Like I said, we're just talking to each other. Getting to know one another more, is all. The way I see it from here, there's nothing wrong with doing that. It would be nice to have someone to talk to about how my day went. Or what I did over the weekend. I'm sure you could use that too, am I wrong?"

As I listen to her, I see the pleading in her eyes. I'm starting to consider this idea even against my better judgement. My heart and loneliness are starting to get the better of me. I also feel her heart tugging on mine. The world as I know it is about to change for better or worse, which I just don't know yet which it will be.

Nodding, I say, "Yeah, I could use someone to talk to about my day for sure. Or heck just to bounce some dinner ideas off of."

"And so what if a little flirting happens," Anne says with a twinkle in her eye.

With a groan I say, "Definitely not, I take enough cold showers because of you as it is."

"Really?"

"Yes, really."

"Because of lil' ol' me?" She feigns surprise.

"Yes, because of lil' ol' you. Wanna see my water bill?" I feign looking around for my bill back at her.

I'm playing with fire, and I know it.

"That bad, eh?" she asks.

"Pretty much."

"Okay, I'll give you a bit of a reprieve," she says. "What was dinner for tonight?"

"I made fettuccine alfredo with prosciutto; it's one of my favorite meals."

"That sounds so good. I wish I had the ingredients to make it tonight."

"There's always Instacart," I say.

"True. Do you cook a lot?"

"I try to as much as I can, but with work sometimes it just isn't possible. How about you?"

"About the same. I try where I can, but sometimes work and life get in the way of that."

"So, what's dinner going to be tonight?"

"I'm not sure, I was thinking a salad or maybe sushi," she says. "There are a couple of good delivery places for both near me."

"Those both sound tasty."

She's glancing down and scrolling on her phone. "I think I'm going to get a mixed greens salad with ahi tuna. Speaking of greens, how's your garden doing so far this year?"

"Pretty good this year. Obviously, I don't get the growing season like you have out west, so I'm super envious of that."

I wonder if I could find a similar house to mine on the water out west? Would it bust my budget? Then I could grow year around.

"Out here, we're lucky that we can get fresh produce from local farmer's markets just about year around. But I can only imagine being able to grow some of your own food."

"It's relaxing and fulfilling to see something that you start from seeds or seedlings turn into something."

"I've always liked plants, but I don't know where to get started with it?"

"I'd say succulents. They're easy. Just water them every once in a while. From there, you could branch out if you want to. If you'd like can email you some suggestions for succulents and other low maintenance houseplants?"

"That would be great!"

"Give me a few days, and I'll get a list sent over to you."

"Oh, no rush at all. Thanks in advance."

"Sure thing."

"Uber Eats is here," she says. "Be right back."

"Okay."

What we're having for dinner? Plants? This is innocent, normal in fact. This could work, couldn't it?

The playlist that I'd forgotten was playing in the background switches to "Make Me Lose Control" just as she comes back into view with her takeout order and a smile.

"Oh, I really like this song." Anne begins to eat her salad.

"Me too; it's one of my favorites."

I think about the lyrics and how they talk about being close to someone and love and the song title. Honestly, my mind needs to distract itself with something else and not focus on the lyrics before this takes a turn in a direction it shouldn't right now.

"How's the salad?"

"Hitting the salad spot tonight."

We talk in between her bites.

"A good salad will do that…god, that sounds so corny. It sounded funnier in my head."

"Ha! It *is* funny. I've always loved your sense of humor."

"Thanks. Sometimes it comes off as way too dry and dumb sounding."

"No, not in the least."

"Thanks for saying that."

"Something to Talk About" starts playing. Great. What the heck is up with this auto-generated playlist tonight? It's killing me.

"Really like the music you're playing tonight. Not trying to drop any hints, are you?"

"Promise it's not intentional. Just the algorithm losing its mind tonight at the most inopportune moment."

"You sure? 'Cause I'm game if you're game?" Anne says with a wink. Salad finished, she closes the empty box.

"Anne, you're killing me," I say with another groan. "That wink is going to be the death of me."

"And why is that?"

"Because it's adorable every time you do it, is why. Just the same way your smile is."

Thank you, Eric Carmen and Bonnie Raitt, for making me to start to lose my resolve. And this is where I begin to cave. I try to not look at how truly stunning she is. How truly perfect she is. The way the waves of her hair fall around her face. How her eyes always twinkle with a smile to them that mirrors those luscious lips. And then the slow throbbing begins.

"No, I am not!"

"You really don't see it, do you?"

"See what?" she says with a look of confusion on her face.

She's being sincere right now and doesn't see her own beauty.

"How utterly gorgeous you are in each and every way." As I'm talking, I see her begin to blush.

"Me? I'm just a plain Jane."

I start ticking things off with my fingers. "You are so much more than just a plain Jane. You're smart, funny, the most creative person I've ever met. And to top it all off, sexy as hell. All of those things together make you just about irresistible. During meetings I try not to stare at you, so I don't come off like a creep. I also just about hang onto every word that you have to say."

"Thank you for all the nice things you've been saying. I can never see myself that way. Ever. I never would have thought your feelings were this strong. You hide them so well. I know I hide mine pretty well too. Just so you know, I was looking at you too. I couldn't take my eyes off of you either."

"Now that last one I wouldn't have ever guessed in a million years. You hide your feelings very well." My mouth is agape in shock. "As for me hiding them, well, you know all the reasons. We've talked about all of them before."

"I'm just thinking about all the time that's been lost for us is all."

"What can never be, can never be lost in the first place."

"But Helen, I ache all the time for you in the dark!" she exclaims.

"And I throb for you right now! But that doesn't mean this can be!" I say back as I run my fingers through my hair in frustration.

"Wait! What?"

"You make me throb all the time," I say in a much softer voice.

"Then, what do we do about this? Personally, I have some ideas, but I've never done them this way before."

She's going *there*, isn't she? I can feel the blush starting from my neck up through my face. Am I ready to do something like *this* with *her* right *now*? I just plow on through like the fool I am.

"I had an ex who had to travel for work at times," I say. "Sometimes we'd both have an itch that needed to be scratched. So, when she'd be gone for a couple of weeks, we'd have video sex sessions. Is that what you're talking about?"

"Bingo! That would be it; I'm hoping it would help take the edge off for both of us. I've done phone sex, but this is a whole different concept for me. I'm really nervous about the whole thing. Over the phone, I'm nervous, don't get me wrong. I was just less so because no one was watching me pleasure myself."

"I think everyone is like that the first time with anything to be honest. Are you still sure you want to do this?"

"Positive. I can't stop thinking about you."

"And I can't stop thinking about you, either. I'm going to move to my bedroom so that I can get more comfortable. I'll try not move the iPad around too much while I walk over there so that it's not jarring on your side of things with the camera view."

"I'm in my living room right now," she says. "I'll try to do the same with my laptop. I moved into my spare guest bedroom a few months ago, so I know I'll have total privacy in there."

"That's good about having privacy; we both should be relaxed so that we can be in the moment with each other. I'm opening my bedroom door right now and turning on the nightstand light."

"Just shut the door to my room and did the same with lighting. I liked the diffused lighting idea from a nightstand light."

"I was going to suggest a little striptease to lighten the tension but to be honest I think that would just make me throb harder which is not what I need right now. What I need is you, to hear your sweet voice."

"I agree with you. I'm barely holding it together right now because of how hard the throbbing is. I need you more, to see your beautiful brown eyes looking at me."

I set my iPad on the bed and in full view of it remove my T-shirt and lounge pants. I watch Anne do the same; she is simply exquisite in every way. Bras come next, then panties. Then there is nothing left but the full view of the beauty that is her body.

Climbing on the bed, I take the iPad and set it down beside me as I lay down on my side so that it's positioned at just the right angle to show most of me. I lean on an elbow and watch Anne do something similar. She is so incredible. Instantly, I'm drenched. I'm pulled from my thoughts by her sexy voice.

"How does this look?" she bashfully asks.

"You look amazing, I'm so wet for you right now. How does my side look?"

"Just as amazing. I can't stop throbbing for you."

I realize I've been unconsciously touching my nipple as a small low moan escapes me.

I see Anne's eyes go wide with desire as she gives an evil grin and starts to stroke one of hers. I hear a whimper fall from her mouth.

"Oh, my god, I'm never going to last at this rate," I say. "This ache is getting so much worse."

"It's almost excruciating at this point."

"I need to start touching myself." Then, I'm moving

down to my pearl as another moan escapes me. All while watching Anne mirror my movements as she also watches me. Our eyes lock on to each other. We each let out a gasp.

"Watching you is such a big turn on for me," I hear her say with a breathy voice.

"This moment has played out quite a few times in my head except we're together and touching each other." I'm starting to writhe on the bed at this point with no control. "I always picture myself stroking your pearl up and down a couple of time. Then on a down stroke entering your core where I stroke your G-spot a couple of times. Then the whole thing starts all over again with your pearl."

"Let's do that right now," Anne pants out as I see her spread her legs wider and start to move her hand in the way I described.

Nodding, I widen my legs and start pleasuring myself all while thinking about and looking at her.

"I can't believe you're here with me right now." I gasp out between moans.

"Neither can I. You know I've had similar fantasies about you, too, right?" Anne breathes out.

"I would have never guessed."

"Believe it."

"I'm so close right now. How close are you?"

"Very."

"I can wait; I want us to cum together. I need for us to cum together," I say longingly.

Everything has become so frantic now. I see the eagerness in her eyes as she starts to squirm on her bed. I feel myself starting to thrust up to meet my fingers.

"We need this," I hear Anne breathlessly utter through the pounding in my ears.

My eyes roll toward her as we both cry out our rapture in unison.

I can't believe I did this and with Anne; it was so amazing.

Turning to her with a smile I say, "That was incredible!"

As she catches her breath I see her nod. "It really was!"

We're now each both propped up on an elbow facing each other

Anne says, "Where do we go from here?"

"Honestly, I don't know."

Chapter Six

SEVERAL WEEKS HAVE PASSED and even though I know for the sake of my job that I shouldn't. I've been talking to Anne every night (and sometimes during the day) since that first night we had cyber sex. She ended up having "the talk" with Jose—who finally agreed that he, too, wasn't happy, and that he, too, wanted an eventual divorce.

Anne and I talk about anything and everything. I already knew we had so much in common with her, but I really never *knew* how much more we had until I started talking to her all the time. We can't get enough of talking with one another. I'm also starting to have thoughts that I didn't think I'd ever have that were this deep. The one word that begins with the letter L, ends with the letter E, and is four letters kind.

"I agree. Potato salad should never just be mustard; you gotta have mayonnaise in there too, or it just doesn't taste right."

"Helen, do you put chips inside your sandwiches?"

"Of course, it's the only way to eat a sandwich!"

"Same here. It just doesn't feel right otherwise."

What Anne doesn't know is that besides talking to her is clicking around on a map of California again, while I'm supposed to be working. Hmm, around Santa Barbara seems like a nice place to visit. There's the coast right there, so beaches. I'll have to check the rental sites and see what a beach house in that area rents for. Question is, how long am I staying there for? A week? A month? Longer? Forever?

"You're so adorable," I say.

"No, that's you."

Forever? Don't put the cart before the horse. You're just taking a little vacation to clear your head so that you can better think about things. Thinking about things? You're thinking about a beach rental in California. Now, who do you know that lives in California? Anne lives in California. You're going to visit Anne and you know it. Stop lying to yourself. But she's just perfect. We have so many things in common, and I'm so attracted to her. And I think she feels the same way about me otherwise, why would she be either on the phone or video chat with me almost twenty-four seven?

I just need to meet her. But is she going to want to meet you? Her talking about it is one thing but you actually showing up in her state is another. There's only one way to find out; I need to book this trip. Before that can happen, I'll have to find some free time on Rhett's calendar. It's been a long time since I've taken any real time off so need to talk with him first ahead of booking anything set in stone.

* * *

It's a little past eight pm, and I'm supposed to video call Anne in a few minutes. I'm still not sure how to broach the subject that a few days ago I booked a beach house in California for a month. Let alone the fact that I want her to visit me there. Like with everything I guess I'll just figure it out.

"Hi, Sweetie!"

"Well, hello there, Hon."

"I booked a beach house in Carpinteria for a month, and I'd like for you to come out and visit me if you can."

Did I just blab that out? I did, didn't I? I gotta stop doing that.

"That sounds fantastic. When did you decide this?"

"I've been mulling it around for a while now and looking up and down the coast on a map trying to find someplace that looked relaxing and quiet. Carpinteria looked like the spot to me. Is it far from you?"

"No, not at all in my part of the valley it's about an hour or so from me. I actually really like that area."

"I've been nervous that you'd say no. I also made sure it was pet friendly for Georgie and Eleni. As well as for Rose and Lilac so that you could bring them if you wanted to."

"That's great. I'll definitely be bringing them with me."

"I also made sure it was a two bedroom so no pressure there either."

"I'm pretty sure that second bedroom won't be being used by us. Maybe the girls but not by us."

"I've been so worried about telling you."

"There's nothing to be worried about, I assure you. Now are you going to be working from there?"

"No, I talked to Rhett. It's been a long time since I've taken a real vacation, so I told him I had the time saved up and that I was taking the full month to recharge. He was fine with it. The engineering manager will be responsible for things while I'm out. There's a lot of different things I need to clear my head about and there's no time like the present. I leave in a couple of weeks."

"I think this is great news. We finally get to meet in-person and be together in the same room for a change, not just on the phone or over video. I'm so excited and surprised by the whole thing. It caught me off guard in a good way."

"Maybe your boss will let you have a week off during that time you could show me some of the sights near there."

"I'm hoping she will, too. I'm also thinking about working from your beach house if that's alright with you."

"It sure is. I had my fingers crossed that you were going to ask that. I'm also anticipating that you'll be there the entire time, but only if you want to."

"Of course, I'd want to! I don't want to waste any second with you so near me."

"Neither do I. Just thinking about us holding each other for the very first time gives me goosebumps. Honestly can't believe I'm actually doing this, that this is really happening. When I think about it, it sounds like something someone else would do."

"You know what it sounds like to me?" she asks. "It sounds like something a person who's known another person for a really long time would do if they wanted to finally meet them in person. That's what it sounds like to me."

"Do you know that you always have a way of making me feel better about myself?"

"I do?"

"Yes, you do. Always."

"Just so you know you do the same for me."

"Do I?" I ask.

"You sure do."

"I never knew. I guess you bring out the best in me. You know what else?"

"What?"

"You're adorable and gorgeous."

"No, that's you."

Inside I'm still a jumble of worry. Am I making the biggest mistake of my life? Will this total thing cost me my heart and my career to boot? My astrological sign is cancer. We cancers don't like coming out of our shells. We sure as hell don't like taking risks. This seems like one big heck of a risk to take on what might feels like the L word, but in reality could just be infatuation. I'm stirred out of my thoughts by Anne's beautiful voice.

"I know you're concerned about us meeting for the first time" she says. "Just believe in us and the fact that everything is going to be just as we've both imagined it in our minds, which is amazing."

"How do you always know what I'm thinking?"

"I just do, so don't worry everything is working out just as it should be. Remember we both want this."

"I will and won't forget. I promise."

Chapter Seven

WELL, the day has finally come, and it couldn't have come sooner. The previous two weeks had to have been the slowest two weeks of my entire life and dragged on forever. I was able to finish my manuscript on the plane ride and got it sent off to Anne for editing and critiquing. I'm interested in her feedback on it. Writing was a much-needed distraction for me and helped calm my nerves on the plane.

Directly after picking up my car rental near the LAX airport, I hit bumper to bumper traffic. For the next forty or so minutes on the 405, I weave in and out of congestion that makes my insides crawl with irritation. Finally, over the hills, I end up in the Valley—the area where Anne lives —and everything opens. There are less cars. From what I can see from the highway, there's more space between buildings and less congestion in general. This area seems more livable than the area around the airport, that's for damn sure; I can see why Anne likes it here in the Valley, and I've hardly seen anything at all.

The rest of my drive is scenic and relaxing with views

of mountains, some farmlands and eventually the ocean. I pass fresh produce stands along the way on the side of the road, not being able to pass them up I stop at some to grab some fruit and vegetables to stock the house with along with some local honey. Since I'm also thirsty I try something, the locals call agua fresca (in Spanish it simply means fresh water) which is a fruit juice-based drink. I get mine from another vendor along the side of the road, opting for a watermelon one.

After about a two-hour drive, I hit the outskirts of Carpinteria and see some farmlands. Technically Carpinteria is a city, but its land area is only 2.6 square miles. It's one of the reasons I picked it; I wanted a small beach town that looked quiet. The other was I hoping from looking at the map that it would be near Anne. The center of the city looks like any other small beach town with quaint shops and restaurants along with some other typical local businesses. Once I start to get into the more residential areas the roads start to narrow. I head toward the beach side and find my rental without any issues and park in the driveway.

First things first, I walk over to the passenger side of the SUV to let Eleni and Georgie out. Even though they'd had pee and water breaks when we'd first gotten off the plane and along the way, it's just easier to get them unloaded first. With the girls in tow, I grab my luggage and grocery bags and head to the house where I unlock the keypad to the front door and step through. The place is an open concept one level with hardwood throughout.

A quick walkthrough shows the kitchen is spacious and stocked with decent pans and spices. The bathrooms have linens, and both have rain showers in each, with the master bath also having a soaker tub big enough for two. The living room has a huge TV hanging on the wall along with a big wood fireplace for those cold beach nights. I spot a set of sliding doors and head through them.

Stepping out through the sliders off the living room the deck is big and has another set of sliders in front of the master bedroom. The first thing I see are clean water bowls near a water spigot. I fill them, and the girls start drinking. The next thing I see are a set of Adirondack chairs with cushions and another that are zero gravity chairs. After the plane ride and drive, I go for one of the zero-g chairs and sink down into it while pulling out my phone. Next on the agenda is an Instacart order with some staples along with some dog food.

Sundries taken care of, my shoes are kicked off as I stare out onto the sand which leads my eyes to the breaking surf of the Pacific ocean. Smelling the warm salt breeze, I begin to relax even more. Shutting my eyes, I let the sounds of the beach and the sun lightly warming my skin lull me into a mid-afternoon nap. After I'm not sure how long, I hear the crunching of gravel along the side of the house leading toward the deck.

"Well, hello there!" I call out as I stand and wait for her to appear on the side of the deck which is beach level.

"It appears that you have the higher ground," she says in her sultry voice as she steps upon the deck, headed toward me with two golden retrievers behind her.

My heart skips a beat as we walk toward each other and meet in the middle. All coherent thought has left my brain and I'm left dumbstruck with no words coming to mind. As panic sets in my body takes over, I walk even nearer and close the gap that was between us, gently pulling her into a warm but firm embrace. One that lets her know that I'm never letting her go. One that says I'm here for her and no one else. As I wrap my arms around her, I feel her doing the same with the same feelings behind it.

I don't know how long we are like that, but it feels like time stops. I don't know when it happens, but one moment, I am holding her and another I am cupping her face and looking into her eyes. After that, I am pouring my soul as our lips meet for the very first time. There is nothing gentle about the kiss; it is everything that has been bottled up between us from the great distance we've shared. It is all the long nights and deeps conversations. It is all the things we have in common.

Most of all, it is all the passion we have built up from getting to know each other. All those things are conveyed into one earth shattering kiss between us. After much tongue swirling and gasps for breath, we finally break feel.

"I see you got my text that I'd landed," I say with a wink as I gasp one of her hands.

"I figured it'd take you about two hours to get here so I left about an hour ago. I figured I'd give you some time to get settled in," she says with a smile.

"I got here, put my luggage and some produce I picked up along the way at some roadside stands near the front door, and headed out back and sat down. Ordered Instacart and promptly nodded off. I think my groceries are out front."

"They're on the front doorstep; I can help you bring them in and help put them away. I need to go back out to my SUV anyway. I brought a bottle of our favorite wine for us and left it in there because I wanted to see you first."

"And I'm glad you did."

"So am I."

After getting everything (including Anne's luggage) brought in and put away, we settle back out on the deck together with the bottle and some glasses. Sitting side by side, holding hands, we talk.

"Anne, I can't believe I'm sitting out here with you."

"It doesn't seem real, does it?"

Pointing out to the beach and waves I say, "I can see why you like it around here. It's so peaceful and relaxing. It seems like it's off the beaten path. Seems like that for some of the parts of the Valley as well for the little that I saw of it on the drive through it. I could also see why you'd like living there, too."

"The farther you get out from LA, the more normal it gets. Southern California really is a great place to live. I'll show you as much as I can with the time you have here so that you have a better understanding about it if you'd like."

"I'd definitely like that if you're willing to do that."

"For sure."

We both glance to our right and see all four pups asleep in a pile together. Smiling at each other, we both chuckle.

"Seems like they're all getting along I'd say," Anne says.

"Sure, looks like it to me, too."

"Oh, before I forget. I got your manuscript. I really liked it. I really liked how you mixed a thriller with a romance. Totally different than what you typically write. I also positively enjoyed the ending with how Jamie came to the rescue with her martial art school who were made up of police, FBI, and hackers who all banded together to bust in and free Rachil on the down low. I also liked how Rachil got to live with one of the martial artist's family who was FBI with the terms that if her actual family said anything they would be turned over to law enforcement for their actual crimes. It really was a different side of you."

"I don't know what else to say except that the writing

just took over and wanted to write a love story. It felt like the right thing to do as I was writing it."

"I really loved what you did."

"Thank you, your opinion really matters to me," I squeeze her hand as I say this.

"That means a lot to me, coming from you." Anne gives my hand a squeeze back with a kiss to it as she says this.

"More importantly, *you* matter to me."

"As do you to me," Anne says as she turns to me and kisses me with everything she has. As our lips part, I see the passion smoldering in her eyes.

"I must say that was well worth the three-thousand-mile trip here and everything I'd dreamt of and more," I say with a laugh.

"Well, there's more where that came from. Want to take this inside?" she says with a wiggle of her eyebrows. Wordlessly standing up I offer my hand down to Anne to steady her as she stands. As we walk through the sliders hand in hand, I whistle over to the dogs to follow us. The pups settle on the living room couches while we head straight for the master.

Walking into the master I turn to Anne. "I've fanaticized about this very moment a thousand times. I'm not going to lie. I'm excited and so very nervous at the same time."

"I've done the same exact thing, and I feel the same exact same way, but I know everything is going to be fine. We both just have a case of the jitters. It'll be okay, I promise."

Turning to face one another, our mouths find the other. First, it's our lips. Then as they open, our tongues swirl around each other in a dance that only we know. As we break apart, I plant feathery kisses on each of her eyelids.

Then on her forehead, and again on her nose, chin, and one on each cheek. I move along one side of her neck, tasting as I move down to her collarbone.

Undressing each other as we move toward the bed our kisses and caresses getting more frantic until we bump up against the side of the bed. By this time, we are down to just bras and panties. Glancing down I stop and take all of Anne's beauty in. From the natural waves and ringlets of her auburn hair and her deep steel blue eyes. To her perfect, gorgeous, stunning body. I take all of it in. Then I notice one small thing.

"Are we both wearing the same *Star Wars* bra and panty set?" I ask with a hint of a chuckle.

Anne stops and looks. "I do believe we are." She laughs and then proceed to pull me in for another kiss.

Guiding Anne to a sitting position on the bed, I kneel and remove her panties with kisses down and up her inner thighs; a moan escapes her lips.

"Don't worry. There'll be more later," I hear myself saying. Running my hand up her sides, I kiss my way up her belly to the front of her bra. Removing her bra, I place gentle kisses between her breasts. Another moan escapes her mouth. This time, I capture it with my own lips.

"Now, it's my turn," Anne says, and the next thing I know I've been pulled onto the bed and Anne is removing my panties and is stroking my slit. I let out a gasp as I throb. "God, you are so wet it's killing me right now."

She removes her fingers and places them into her mouth. Still not done, she then reaches into my bra and caresses a nipple while removing my bra.

"I need you now," I say with a whine to my voice.

"I need you, too."

We both start to stroke each other's pearls and steal our moans with kisses.

"It feels so good to finally be able to touch you in person and not just imagine it," I say, lengthening my strokes so that I can also reach and rub Anne's G-spot.

Anne gasps and begins to mirror my movements, "Please don't stop what you're doing. It's hitting everything."

"Don't worry I won't. Not until you cum. I promise," I pant out. I feel both of us tighten up as we cry out our release in unison.

Anne lays her head on my shoulder as our heartbeats start to slow.

"It was everything I'd thought it would be and more," she says.

"I feel the same way," I say as I kiss the top of her head while I run my fingers through her hair. Looking down at her I begin to stammer. "Anne, I've been having feelings about you that I feel that are too soon for me. I..." I bite down on my lip, afraid to say the words, but ready to say them, nonetheless. "I love you, Anne."

"I love you too," she cuts in to say, "and I have since we really started talking to each other outside of work. I didn't want to say anything because I didn't want to scare you."

"You do, too?" I say with surprise and joy in my voice. "I was so scared to tell you how I was starting to feel." I look down and her and hold her even closer to me.

"I get it," she says. "It's a hard thing to bring up the very first time because you don't know how the other person feels."

"Exactly, I was so afraid I was going to ruin something before it even had a chance to blossom. I've also had a lot of other things on my mind, too. So, I was worried that those things might be clouding my vision as well."

"What other things? Hon, you can talk to me about anything."

"I've been thinking about making some life changes," I say. "I reached out to someone I know over at Atlas Technologies. His name is Ezra. I wanted to see if they had any openings; it turns out that they do. I interviewed for a remote management position about a week and a half ago. They called to offer me the job, just as I was getting on the plane. I asked them for a few days to think it over before getting back to them; they were okay with that since it's such a big decision."

"Wow, that really is huge."

"It is. I've been getting stagnant over at Cosmic. I've also been thinking about selling my house and moving somewhere warmer."

"You have?"

"For real. I'm getting tired of dealing with the cold winters."

"I could understand how that'd be hard to deal with after a while for sure."

"Would you want to take over as manager if I were to leave?"

"Me?"

"Yes, you. I think you'd make a great manager and you already have shown great leadership skills. All I'd have to do is put in a good word to Rhett and the job would be yours."

"Really? I'd never actually saw myself as one until now."

"Neither did I until I was one. Plus, if we're to be together we can't work for each other. Another reason why I think I'm going to take the job with Atlas. I also just want to be doing something different."

"If I have any questions, will you help me?"

"Of course, I will, my love!"

"Then, yes, please talk to Rhett about me taking over

for you. I don't know how well I'll do since your shoes are big shoes to fill, but I'll have you at my side to help guide me."

"You're a natural and will do just fine without my help, but I'll be there just in case you ever need me."

"Oh, hey, I never did ask. Where are you considering moving?"

I grin, waggling my brows again for good measure. "I think around here. Will you help me find a house that'll fit us plus four dogs on the beach? That is, if you and your girls are willing to move in with us?"

"Of course, we are!"

"Oh, one other thing."

"Yes?"

"I think I know what my next story is going to be about."

"What's it going to be about?"

"A boss who falls madly in love with her younger, beautiful employee. I think it's going to be an age gap trope."

"I love the idea."

"So do I."

About the Author

Artemed Sullivan is a Los Angeles based author who originally hails from the Northeast. She's lived in California long enough to understand what it means to be "California cold."

When she's not writing or reading, she can be found geeking out over something nerdy.

Also by Artemed Sullivan

Ghosting the Blind Date

Christmas Party on Hanukkah

Made in the USA
Las Vegas, NV
31 October 2023

80034576R00049